## C LOWRY

# Deception Tide a Declassified File

Copyright © 2025 by C Lowry

*All rights reserved. No part of this publication may be reproduced, stored or transmitted in any form or by any means, electronic, mechanical, photocopying, recording, scanning, or otherwise without written permission from the publisher. It is illegal to copy this book, post it to a website, or distribute it by any other means without permission.*

*First edition*

*This book was professionally typeset on Reedsy.
Find out more at reedsy.com*

# Contents

| | |
|---|---:|
| DECEPTION TIDE | 1 |
| Chapter 2 | 6 |
| Chapter 3 | 11 |
| Chapter 4 | 16 |
| Chapter 5 | 31 |
| Chapter 6 | 36 |
| Chapter 7 | 42 |
| Chapter 8 | 48 |
| Chapter 9 | 54 |
| Chapter 10 | 60 |
| Chapter 11 | 66 |
| Chapter 12 | 72 |

# DECEPTION TIDE

The Florida heat settled in early, thick and suffocating, turning the marina basin into a simmering stew of diesel fumes, salt, and the faint, discouraging smell of decay from the mangroves fringing the far shore. Two months had passed since Sully dropped me back here, back at the Sea Witch. Two months of letting the sun bake the stiffness out of muscles that still remembered Zukhov's yacht and the bullets too well. Two months of replacing damaged teak, tuning an engine that sounded rougher than I felt, and trying like hell to look like just another slightly down-at-heel boat bum enjoying his semi-retirement.

It wasn't working. The peace felt thin, brittle. My reflection in the cabin porthole showed the new lines etched around my eyes, the silver creeping faster into my hair. The warrants were still out there, a quiet hum of static beneath the surface of everyday life. And the piece of paper Sully had given me, the one with the cryptic coordinates for a supposed dead drop in Okeechobee County, sat tucked away in a waterproof container, mocking me with its unanswered questions. Varga's last play? Zukhov's trap? I couldn't decide, and inertia, mixed with a healthy dose of self-preservation, kept me moored here, sanding brightwork and watching the mullet jump.

Restless. That was the word. Like a caged animal that had forgotten the feel of the bars until it paced into one again. My bank account, propped up by the emergency cash Sully provided, was dwindling faster than the tide. Peace was expensive. Trouble, inconveniently, often paid better.

The burner phone Sully had given me, a bland grey slab of untraceable anonymity, chirped softly from its charging cradle below deck. It wasn't Sully's check-in time. In the two months I'd had it, it had only rung twice, both times Sully verifying secure comms. This was different. A message notification icon glowed on the dark screen.

My gut tightened. Nobody should have this number except Sully. I carried the phone up to the cockpit, glancing around the marina – sleepy, midday quiet, just old Pete varnishing the rail on his ketch three slips down, and a couple of charter boats prepping for the afternoon run. Still, my hand felt clammy as I tapped the screen.

The message was text-only, displayed within a self-destructing encrypted wrapper that dissolved moments after I opened it. No sender ID, no traceable metadata according to the phone's built-in security software. Just cold, concise text:

Kincaid. Your reputation precedes you, despite recent complications. Require your unique skills for retrieval operation. Non-negotiable fee: 500k USD. Half on acceptance, half on completion. Target: Stolen bearer documents, sensitive corporate nature. Location: Hidden within Santuario Verde Ecotourism Reserve, Osa Peninsula, Costa Rica. High security, low profile essential. Reply YES via secure relay channel 7 within 1 hour to accept. Further instructions follow. Silence implies refusal. Consider carefully. Exposure is not an option.

I read it again. Then a third time. Costa Rica. Stolen

documents. Half a million dollars. Anonymous client using military-grade encryption on a phone number only Sully should have. Every alarm bell I possessed was clanging like a fire station next door to a foundry.

Santuario Verde. I didn't know it, but Costa Rica, the Osa Peninsula... that meant jungle. Dense, remote, crawling with things that bite, sting, or just plain disappear you. An "eco-tourism sanctuary" could mean anything from legitimate research station to cartel hideaway to spook training ground. And "stolen documents" was usually code for something far more volatile than corporate secrets – intel, access codes, kill lists.

Who was the client? Someone who knew my real name, knew about my "recent complications" (a delicate way of saying 'framed for murder and shot to pieces on a rogue arms dealer's yacht'), knew how to reach this specific phone, and had half a million dollars to throw at a high-risk retrieval. Could it be Thorne, trying a back channel now that Pym was gone? Unlikely; this felt colder, more professional. Zukhov? Setting an elaborate trap? Possible. Croft? Trying to retrieve something incriminating? Also possible. Or someone new entirely, someone from the deeper shadows Sully hinted at?

Five hundred thousand dollars. Enough to disappear properly, buy a new boat under a new name somewhere far away where Florida warrants didn't reach. Enough to finance my own hunt for Zukhov or Croft, if I was feeling particularly suicidal. Or enough to get me killed in a Costa Rican swamp.

The sun beat down on the deck. I could smell the creosote on the pilings, hear the gentle lapping of water against the hull. Simple sounds. Peaceful sounds. The life I thought I wanted. But the restlessness was still there, a low thrum beneath the surface. And the money... the money was a powerful lure for a man whose options were dwindling.

The Okeechobee dead drop felt like poking a sleeping snake. This Costa Rica job felt like diving into a shark tank wearing chum-soaked shorts. But it was action. It was a direction, however dangerous. And maybe, just maybe, it was a chance to get far away from the ghosts of Pym and Fins, far from the reach of Florida law and Zukhov's lingering threat.

Could Sully have compromised the number? No. Not Sully. Which meant someone else had serious capabilities. Capabilities that might make them a dangerous client, but also potentially a powerful one. Retrieve documents. No mention of wetwork, just extraction. Relatively clean, if you ignored the anonymous client, the jungle setting, and the certainty that whoever currently held the documents wouldn't give them up easily.

Exposure is not an option. My exposure or theirs? Probably both.

I looked at the phone. Forty minutes left on the timer. Costa Rica. Palm trees, volcanoes, toucans... and probably razor wire, motion sensors, and men with guns who didn't care about the local endangered species list.

Half a million.

I took a deep breath, the humid Florida air feeling heavy, stagnant. Time to trade one kind of swamp for another. I navigated the phone's secure interface to relay channel 7, the screen glowing starkly in the bright sunlight. My thumb hovered over the keypad. It was madness. A trap. A fool's errand.

I typed: YES

The single word transmitted, vanishing into the ether. Seconds later, the phone chirped again. Another encrypted message, just as anonymous.

Accepted. Stand by for secure wire transfer confirmation:

250k USD. Initial logistics follow within 1 hour. Maintain this channel exclusively. Burn after reading.

The message dissolved. I stood there in the cockpit of the Sea Witch, the sun hot on my face, the familiar sounds of the marina suddenly distant. The tide was turning, pulling me out again, away from the deceptive calm of the Florida coast, towards the deeper, unknown waters of Costa Rica. I had a feeling the deception wasn't just in the tides this time.

## Chapter 2

The air that hit me stepping off the small propeller plane onto the tarmac at Puerto Jiménez wasn't the familiar, sticky blanket of South Florida. This was different. Heavier, somehow, thick with the smells of damp earth, exotic blossoms, diesel fumes, and something else – the raw, green, fecund scent of serious jungle breathing down the neck of the small coastal town. The heat had teeth here. Cicadas shrieked from unseen trees with manic intensity, a sound that burrowed under your skin. Florida's heat felt tired, worn out; this felt aggressive, intensely alive.

My new identity, Thomas Callahan, supposedly a freelance photographer scouting locations, breezed through the sleepy airport formalities. According to the encrypted instructions that followed the wire transfer, Callahan had a reservation for a battered but functional Toyota Land Cruiser at a dusty rental lot near the harbor, and a booking at a cluster of simple wooden cabins called 'Cabinas El Tucán' just outside town. Anonymous, low-key, blend-with-the-backpackers standard procedure.

Driving the rattling Land Cruiser through Puerto Jiménez, I felt the eyes. Maybe it was just the natural curiosity of a small town seeing a new Gringo face. Maybe it was the accumulated paranoia from Zukhov's island and being framed for murder. But the way a dockworker leaning against a piling paused his conversation to watch me pass, the reflection of a nondescript sedan glimpsed twice in my rearview mirror on different streets, the man reading a newspaper on a park bench whose gaze lingered a little too long... it set my teeth on edge. Experience had taught me to trust the prickle on the back of my neck. Someone was watching. My anonymous client's operation wasn't as low profile as they thought, or someone else was already tracking the stolen documents.

Cabinas El Tucán were basic but clean, tucked away down a rutted dirt road, surrounded by towering vegetation dripping with recent rain. Each cabin stood separate, offering a degree of privacy. I checked in, paid cash for three nights – Callahan needed time to 'scout' – and tossed my duffel onto the simple bed. The instructions specified the initial contact procedure: Be at Cantina El Perezoso, a known waterfront spot in town, at precisely 4 PM. Order a bottle of Imperial beer and ask, in Spanish, if they have gallo pinto for dinner tonight, even though gallo pinto was strictly a breakfast dish. The contact would approach my table.

Cantina El Perezoso – The Sloth Cantina – lived up to its name. Open-air, overlooking the muddy waters of the Golfo Dulce, ceiling fans stirred the humid air with lazy indifference. A few locals nursed beers at the rough wooden bar, ignoring the handful of sunburnt tourists picking at plates of fried fish. Reggae music drifted tinny and distorted from old speakers. I chose a table near the back, partial view of the entrance, partial view of the street outside. Ordered my Imperial, waited for the waitress to bring it, then asked my stupid question about the gallo pinto. She gave me a puzzled look, shrugged, and wandered off.

Fifteen minutes crawled by. The beer was cold, sweating onto the rough wood. The reggae grated. The feeling of being watched intensified. I scanned the street again. The nondescript sedan wasn't visible, but a motorcycle with a lone rider wearing a dark helmet had parked fifty yards down, the rider seemingly just waiting, observing the cantina entrance.

Then, a man slid into the chair opposite me. Local. Tico. Maybe forty, thin face etched with worry, damp patches darkening his guayabera shirt despite the fans. His eyes darted nervously around the cantina before settling on me. He didn't offer a name.

"You are Callahan?" he whispered, leaning forward, his voice tight.

I nodded slowly. "You were expecting me?"

"My associate... the one who arranged this... said you would come." He licked his lips, his gaze flicking towards the street again. "This is dangerous. More dangerous than they told me."

"Most things are," I said. "The documents?"

"Sí. They are at the sanctuary. Santuario Verde." He leaned closer, dropping his voice even lower. "But it is not what it seems, señor. Not just monkeys and birds. There are guards. Men with guns, not park rangers. They watch everything."

"What kind of guards?"

"Hard men. Not Ticos. Foreigners. Military types." He wiped sweat from his upper lip with a trembling finger. "They arrived months ago. Took over the sanctuary administration building, restricted access to the deep reserve areas. The director, Dr. Ramirez... he vanished."

This tracked with the need for a retrieval specialist, not just a sneak thief. But who were these military types? Zukhov's mercs, repositioned after the yacht fiasco? Or another group entirely? "Who are they, Mateo?" I took a guess, using the name stitched almost invisibly onto his shirt pocket.

His eyes widened slightly in fear that I knew his name. "I... I don't know their names. Only the name whispered among the staff who stayed... 'Jaguar'. He runs it. Cold man. Very dangerous." He pushed a folded napkin across the table. "Coordinates. A weak point in the perimeter fence near the old research station. It is all I know. All I want to know."

Jaguar. The name meant nothing, but the description fit the kind of operation Zukhov might run. "Who has the documents? Where within the sanctuary?"

"I don't know!" His voice cracked, attracting a glance from the bartender. He visibly pulled himself together. "Ramirez had them, I think. Before he disappeared. Maybe in his office? The administration building? I cannot go there. Nobody can, without Jaguar's permission." He stood up abruptly, scraping his chair back. "That is all. I did what I was paid for. I must go."

"Wait," I started, but he was already walking quickly towards the cantina entrance, almost running, desperation radiating from him. He stepped out into the late afternoon sunlight filtering through the dusty street.

He made it five steps.

There was no loud bang. Just a soft phut, almost lost in the screech of cicadas and the thumping reggae bassline. Mateo stumbled, a small dark stain blossoming suddenly on the front of his guayabera. His hand went to his chest, confusion and surprise on his face. He took one more wavering step, then collapsed onto the dusty sidewalk like a puppet with its strings cut.

Silence fell in the cantina for a beat. Then, a woman screamed. Patrons scrambled back from the entrance. The motorcyclist down the street kicked his engine to life with a sudden roar and sped away, disappearing around the corner before anyone could properly register what had happened.

I didn't move for a second, frozen, watching Mateo's body lie still in the dust. The surveillance wasn't passive. They knew about the meeting. They waited until he delivered his information, however minimal, then eliminated the loose end. Efficient. Ruthless.

My chair scraped back as I stood, dropping enough colones on the table to cover the beer and then some. No point sticking around for the local police. They wouldn't find the shooter, and they'd find me – a Gringo stranger who was the last person seen talking to the dead man. I walked calmly, deliberately, out the back entrance of the cantina, slipping into the narrow alleyway behind it, forcing myself not to run.

My heart hammered against my ribs. Mateo dead. Jaguar. Armed mercs at a supposedly peaceful sanctuary. Documents important enough to kill for, being retrieved for a client I knew nothing about. The half-million dollar payday suddenly felt like blood money earned in advance.

Reaching the Land Cruiser, parked two blocks away, I slid behind the wheel, hands unsteady. The heat inside the vehicle was stifling. I started the engine, the rattling diesel sounding reassuringly normal in a situation that was anything but. I pulled out into the street, driving slowly, obeying traffic laws I barely noticed, my eyes constantly scanning mirrors, side streets, faces.

The welcome party was over. The real dangers of Costa Rica were just beginning. And Santuario Verde, the Green Sanctuary, now sounded less like a refuge and more like a well-camouflaged killing ground. The documents were there. And so was Jaguar. Time to head into the jungle.

# Chapter 3

The battered Land Cruiser chewed up the miles, leaving the relatively civilized veneer of Puerto Jiménez behind, plunging deeper into the Osa Peninsula's humid embrace. The paved road gave way to graded dirt, then quickly degenerated into deeply rutted tracks of red mud carved through walls of impenetrable green. Towering trees formed a dense canopy overhead, filtering the sunlight into a dim, steamy twilight at ground level. The air grew thicker, wetter, buzzing with insects the size of my thumb. Howler monkeys roared in the distance, a primal sound that seemed to shake the very air. This wasn't the Everglades, flat and sprawling; this was vertical, tangled, ancient jungle, swallowing the narrow track whole. Twice, I had to ford streams where dubious-looking log bridges had collapsed, the Land Cruiser slipping and sliding, threatening to bog down in the mud.

All the while, my mind raced. Mateo dead. Jaguar. Mercenaries guarding an ecotourism reserve. Stolen documents worth killing for. An anonymous client paying half a million. It smelled bad, the kind of bad that clings to you long after you leave. The kind of bad I specialized in, apparently. The surveillance in town meant they knew someone was coming, tipped off perhaps by the same client who hired me, or maybe they just monitored everything connected to Mateo. Either way, walking into Santuario Verde felt less like infiltration and more like volunteering for target practice.

Late afternoon found me near the coordinates Mateo had provided, pulled off the main track onto an overgrown spur road marked with a faded sign mentioning an 'Estación Biológica Experimental' – the old research station. According to the reserve map included in Callahan's flimsy cover documentation, this area was officially closed to visitors due to 'sensitive ecosystem regeneration'. Convenient.

I parked the Land Cruiser deep under the cover of broad-leafed strangler figs, camouflaging it as best I could with cut branches, then gathered my gear: a lightweight pack with water, basic medical supplies, night vision goggles, lock picks, my silenced pistol, spare ammo, and a sturdy machete I'd bought back in town. Thomas Callahan, nature photographer, was about to do some very unnatural trespassing.

Following Mateo's napkin map, I pushed into the dense undergrowth paralleling the main perimeter fence line. The fence itself wasn't overly imposing – standard chain link, maybe eight feet high, topped with a few strands of barbed wire – but I spotted sophisticated vibration sensors attached at intervals, along with tiny, well-camouflaged cameras tucked into the foliage. This wasn't designed to keep monkeys out; it was meant to keep people out, or at least, know when they tried to get in.

Mateo's weak point was exactly where he'd indicated: a narrow gully, eroded by rainwater runoff, that passed under the fence line. Years of erosion had created a gap nearly two feet high, partially obscured by overgrown roots and ferns. Sensors weren't feasible in the constantly shifting mud of the gully floor. I lay flat, scanning the area, listening. Nothing but the incessant thrum of the jungle. Moving slowly, carefully, I wriggled through the muddy gap, scraping my pack, emerging inside the Santuario Verde reserve. The air felt different on this side. Colder, somehow. Tenser.

My immediate surroundings matched the 'closed research station' cover. A few dilapidated wooden structures, roofs sagging, paint peeling, slowly being reclaimed by vines and strangler figs. Overgrown experimental plots marked with faded scientific tags. It looked convincingly abandoned. But as I moved cautiously deeper, following a barely discernible path leading away from the station towards the reserve's interior, the signs began to change.

The path became clearer, better maintained than any public trail, the undergrowth cut back with precision. I found footprints in a muddy patch – not the casual hikers or rubber boots of researchers, but the distinct, deep tread of military-style combat boots. Multiple sets, moving with purpose. Further on, faint but unmistakable sounds drifted through the trees – rhythmic grunts, the thud of impacts, too regular for animal noises.

Veering off the path, moving parallel through the dense jungle, I climbed a small rise overlooking a hidden clearing. My breath caught. Below me wasn't a research area or a birdwatching platform. It was an obstacle course. Ropes, climbing walls, parallel bars, tire pits – well-used, maintained, clearly designed for serious physical conditioning. Beyond it, partially hidden by another stand of trees, I could just make out the edge of what looked like a firing range backstop, though I heard no shots – likely using suppressors or operating on a strict schedule.

This wasn't just a sanctuary guarded by mercs. This was the operation. Mateo hadn't known the half of it. Santuario

Verde was a front, a perfectly isolated, camouflaged location for training paramilitary recruits. Zukhov's people? Or someone else entirely drawn to this remote corner of Central America?

My mission parameters shifted drastically. Retrieving documents from a research director's office was one thing. Infiltrating an active, clandestine military training camp was a whole different level of insanity. But the documents were still the objective. And according to Mateo, Dr. Ramirez's office was likely in the main administration building.

Following the direction indicated on the Callahan map for the 'Visitor Center & Administration', I continued my stealthy progress, hyper-aware of every sound, every shadow. The vegetation grew less wild, transitioning into more manicured landscaping – suspicious in itself this deep in the reserve. I saw more guards now, patrolling in pairs, moving with disciplined alertness, carrying modern assault rifles, communicating via earpieces. They wore simple khaki fatigues, no insignia, but their bearing screamed professional soldier, not eco-guard. They weren't Ticos. Eastern European, maybe? Hard to tell from a distance.

Finally, through a screen of decorative bamboo, I saw it. The administration complex. Not the rustic wooden structure depicted in the tourist brochures. This was a low, bunker-like building, reinforced concrete painted jungle green, tinted windows, multiple antennas bristling from the roof. It sat in the center of a cleared area, offering no easy approach routes. Security cameras swept the perimeter. The main entrance was guarded by two more mercs.

This was Jaguar's den. Getting inside would require more than just lock picks. As I watched from concealment, a group of about twenty men, also in khakis, emerged from a pathway leading from the direction of the obstacle course. They moved in formation, heading towards a cluster of newer, barrack-style buildings tucked away behind the admin complex – buildings definitely not on any official map. Trainees, reporting back after drills.

The scale of it hit me then. This wasn't a handful of guards protecting a stash. This was an organized, operational base, training dozens, maybe hundreds, of paramilitary fighters. For what purpose? Destabilization, as Varga had uncovered before Zukhov's auction? Insurgency? Terrorism?

The stolen documents suddenly seemed even more critical. What secrets did Ramirez possess that warranted this level of security, this kind of operation built around it? Finding them just got exponentially harder, and infinitely more important. I settled deeper into the shadows, the humid jungle air thick with unspoken menace. Phase one – infiltration – was complete. Phase two – finding the documents inside a hostile military camp – was about to begin. And the odds, already long, had just gotten considerably worse.

# Chapter 4

Darkness fell quickly under the jungle canopy, the transition from oppressive daylight to profound night happening almost instantly, like a switch being thrown. The air grew marginally cooler but no less thick, and the cacophony of daytime insects was replaced by the chirps, croaks, and rustles of nocturnal creatures, punctuated by the unnerving shriek of something I couldn't identify deep in the woods. From my concealed position overlooking the administration building, the scene took on a different character. Security lights cast pools of harsh white glare, creating pockets of impenetrable shadow between them. The guard patrols seemed tighter, more alert, their flashlights cutting sharp beams through the humid air.

My window of opportunity would be the shift change, scheduled for 2100 hours according to the pattern I'd observed. A brief period of overlapping patrols, radio chatter, maybe slightly lowered vigilance as one group handed off to another. My target was a ventilation shaft grille low on the building's less-guarded rear wall, partially obscured by overgrown ornamental shrubs. Big enough to squeeze through if I could get the grille off quietly. Risky, but less exposed than trying the doors or windows.

As 2100 approached, I began my slow crawl through the damp grass and decorative plantings, moving from shadow to shadow,

## CHAPTER 4

every rustle of leaves sounding like a gunshot in the tense silence. The humidity plastered my clothes to my skin; sweat dripped into my eyes, stinging. I reached the cover of the shrubs near the ventilation shaft, paused, listening intently. Heard the crunch of boots on the gravel path nearby as one patrol passed, their voices murmuring in a language that sounded vaguely Slavic. Waited until they moved on.

I reached for the grille, testing its fastenings – standard screws, corroded by the damp climate. My multi-tool made short work of them, the grating sound seeming deafeningly loud to my own ears. Just as I eased the grille away from the opening, a faint scrape came from inside the shaft.

I froze, hand hovering over the grip of my pistol. My heart hammered against my ribs. Had I triggered an internal sensor? Was someone waiting inside?

Then, a figure emerged from the black opening of the shaft, moving with impossible silence, wriggling out feet first. Not one of the bulky mercs. Smaller, leaner, dressed in dark, practical clothing that blended with the shadows. As the figure straightened up in the meager light filtering through the shrubs, I saw it was a woman. She moved with the fluid grace of someone highly trained, her eyes immediately scanning the surroundings, her hand holding a small, suppressed pistol, held low but ready.

Our eyes met in the gloom. Surprise flickered across her face, quickly replaced by wary tension mirroring my own. We were maybe five feet apart, both armed, both caught completely off guard. Neither of us could afford the noise of a gunshot.

"Fancy meeting you here," I whispered, keeping my own weapon trained loosely in her direction.

Her pistol remained steady, aimed at my center mass. "Who are you?" Her voice was low, controlled, with a faint accent I couldn't immediately place – maybe European, maybe Israeli.

"Just admiring the landscaping," I replied. "You?"

"Checking the air conditioning," she retorted dryly, her eyes narrowed, assessing me. "You don't look like one of Jaguar's boys."

The name Mateo had given me. Using it was a risk, could mark me as an outsider, but also might serve as a password. "Jaguar?" I kept my tone neutral. "Runs a tight ship, doesn't he? Especially for an ecotourism reserve."

Her gaze sharpened. A flicker of something – recognition? Calculation? "You know the name." It wasn't a question. "Who sent you? Who do you work for?"

"Let's just say I'm looking for something that belonged to Dr. Ramirez. Something his new management seems keen on keeping." I watched her reaction closely.

She hesitated, her pistol dipping almost imperceptibly. "Ramirez's research?"

"Could be," I allowed. "Seems valuable."

"Valuable enough to get people killed." Her eyes flicked towards the main path, listening. "We can't stay here. They do random sweeps." She made a decision. "Follow me. Stay low. Make a sound, and I shoot you myself." She turned and slipped back towards the deeper shadows at the edge of the manicured area, moving with incredible speed and silence.

Against my better judgment, I followed, replacing the vent grille quickly, hoping it wouldn't be noticed immediately. She led me away from the admin building, deeper into the overgrown, unlit area bordering the jungle proper, finally stopping in a dense thicket that offered complete concealment.

"Alright," she said, turning to face me, pistol still ready but not quite aimed. "Talk. Fast. Who are you?"

"Call me Callahan. I was hired to retrieve Ramirez's documents. That's all I know."

"Hired by who?"

"Client prefers anonymity. You?"

She studied me for another long moment. "My name is Elena. I was working with Dr. Ramirez. Officially, cataloging reptile species for the sanctuary." Her cover was thin, but plausible enough. "When Jaguar and his people arrived, Ramirez became... concerned. He hid his recent research data. Then he vanished. I stayed on, pretending to continue my work, trying to find out what happened to him, what happened to his data."

"And what have you found?"

"That this place," she gestured vaguely towards the hidden camp, "is run by professionals. Mercenaries. Highly trained, well-equipped. They're training recruits here, dozens of them. And they answer to someone much bigger."

"Zukhov?" I asked quietly, testing the name.

Her head snapped up, eyes widening in surprise, suspicion flaring again. "How do you know that name?"

"Let's just say I've run across his associates before. In Florida." The yacht, the arsenal, the framing – I didn't need to elaborate. If she knew Zukhov, she knew the syndicate.

Elena let out a slow breath, finally lowering her pistol, though her hand stayed near it. "Okay, Callahan. Maybe we do have a problem in common. Zukhov's syndicate, yes. They provide the muscle, the logistics. Jaguar reports to them. This training camp... it's part of their expansion into Central America. Destabilization is the goal."

So, the pattern continued. Zukhov, or the syndicate he represented, wasn't just dealing arms; they were training armies, fomenting chaos. "And Ramirez's documents? What's so important about them?"

"I don't know exactly," she admitted. "He was frantic before he disappeared. Said it was proof. Something that could expose the entire operation, not just here, but the financial network behind it."

Croft. The phantom financier. The documents might be the key to linking him, and others like him, directly to Zukhov's field operations. "Where did he hide them? You said his office?"

"That's my best guess. He spent most of his time there. But getting inside..." She shook her head. "Security is tight. Electronic locks, pressure plates, constant surveillance inside. Jaguar uses it as his command center now."

"I came through the vent shaft," I said. "Maybe there's another way in."

"Maybe," she conceded. "But we're wasting time. And now that we know about each other..."

"Yeah," I finished. "One of us trips an alarm, we both pay the price." A reluctant alliance. The worst kind, built on necessity and mutual suspicion. "Look, Elena. I don't trust you any farther than I can throw that Land Cruiser I parked back there. And I'm guessing the feeling's mutual."

"You guess right, Callahan."

"But we both want what's in Ramirez's office. You want proof; I want to complete my job and get paid, assuming my client isn't the one who just tried to kill my contact back in town."

"Mateo?" she asked sharply. "He's dead?"

"Silenced pistol, right after he talked to me."

Elena cursed softly in a language I didn't recognize. "They're cleaning house. Which means they know someone is coming for the documents." She looked at me, her expression grim. "Temporary truce? We work together to get inside the admin building, find Ramirez's office, get the data. Then we figure out the rest."

"Agreed," I said. "Temporary. We watch each other's backs, but we watch each other just as close. Deal?"

"Deal." She gave a curt nod. "Night is our best cover. We move now, try to get access while the graveyard shift settles in. Follow my lead; I know the blind spots in the camera coverage near the west wing."

She melted back into the shadows, and I followed, the uneasy truce hanging heavy in the humid air. Teaming up with an unknown undercover agent inside a hostile paramilitary camp run by the same syndicate that wanted me dead... it wasn't the smartest plan. But it was the only one I had. The jungle pressed close, hiding dangers seen and unseen, and the fortified building ahead held secrets worth killing for. Ours, or theirs.

"Ready?" Elena whispered, her voice barely audible above the drone of insects outside. We were crouched by a low maintenance hatch set into the rear wall of the administration building, concealed by thick, flowering bushes that filled the night air with a cloying sweetness. The harsh security lights didn't quite penetrate this deep into the decorative planting.

"As I'll ever be," I murmured back, scanning the shadows one last time. "You're sure about this hatch? Looks like it hasn't been opened since Cortez."

"It bypasses the main door sensors and the pressure plates in the immediate entryway. Leads to a utility crawlspace adjacent to the west wing offices. Ramirez showed it to me once, said it was an emergency egress from the old generator room before they built this monstrosity." She produced a thin, specialized tool. "Standard magnetic lock, easily overridden if you know how." She inserted the tool, manipulated it briefly, and the hatch clicked open with unnerving loudness in the relative quiet.

"After you," I gestured. No point arguing chivalry when dealing with potential booby traps or waiting guards.

She gave me a look that could curdle milk but slid silently through the opening into the pitch blackness beyond. I followed, pulling the hatch closed behind us as gently as possible. The air inside was cool, stale, smelling of dust and ozone. We were in a narrow crawlspace, pipes and conduits lining the walls. Elena clicked on a penlight shielded with a red filter, casting an eerie, limited glow.

"Stay close," she breathed. "There are infrared beams in the main corridors, tied into the cameras. We need to reach the central records office – Ramirez kept hard copies of almost everything there, paranoid about digital failures. If his research notes exist anywhere, they'll be there."

We moved like ghosts through the building's hidden veins, Elena navigating by memory, me watching our backs, pistol ready, every creak of the structure, every hum of machinery setting my nerves on edge. Twice, we froze as heavy footsteps echoed from the corridor beyond the thin wall, waiting until they passed. It felt like crawling through the guts of some sleeping concrete beast.

Finally, Elena stopped, pointing her dim red light at a ventilation grille higher up on the crawlspace wall. "This looks into the records office hallway. Should be clear this time of night, but check."

I eased up, peered through the grille. A long, sterile corridor stretched left and right, lit by dim overhead emergency lights.

## CHAPTER 4

Empty. "Clear."

Getting out of the crawlspace and into the office itself involved bypassing another electronic lock on a heavy fire door – Elena handled that with unnerving speed – and then disabling the office door's simpler magnetic lock and pressure sensor. We slipped inside, closing the door silently behind us.

The records office wasn't what I expected. Less dusty archives, more modern command hub. Banks of servers hummed quietly along one wall. Multiple workstations sat dark. Filing cabinets lined another wall, but they looked too standard for Ramirez's critical research. In the center of the room, a large digital mapping table, currently dark, dominated the space. This wasn't just where records were kept; this was where Jaguar, or someone high up, worked.

"Ramirez's specific project files wouldn't be out here," Elena whispered, moving towards a workstation. "He had a private safe, supposedly fireproof, somewhere in his main office down the hall. But maybe the access logs..." She began carefully working on the keyboard, using what looked like a sophisticated decryption device plugged into a USB port.

While she worked the digital angle, I did the physical sweep. Checked the filing cabinets – personnel files for the mercs (code-names mostly), training schedules, requisitions for ammunition and supplies – confirming the scale of the camp but nothing on Ramirez or the documents. No obvious safes. I moved towards the large mapping table. Its surface was dark, but a faint power light glowed on the console. Maybe it held recent operational data.

"Anything?" I asked Elena, keeping my voice low.

"Firewalls are serious," she muttered, frowning at the screen. "Military grade. Trying a backdoor exploit Ramirez mentioned once..."

I examined the mapping table console. No obvious power switch, likely controlled remotely or from a master terminal. But there was a small slot, like for a data card. And tucked slightly underneath, almost out of sight, was a slim black data card reader, still plugged in. Someone had forgotten, or been interrupted while using it. Beside it lay a single data card, looking innocuous. Curiosity, or maybe just a hunch born of desperation, made me pick it up. No label. I glanced at Elena, still engrossed in her decryption attempt. Slipping the card into the reader felt like a gamble, but sitting idle wasn't helping.

The large screen above the table flickered to life, startling both of us. Elena spun around, hand reaching for her weapon. "What did you do?"

"Found a data card," I said, pointing.

The screen resolved into a detailed topographical map, not of Costa Rica, but of the northern triangle of Central America – Guatemala, Honduras, El Salvador. Overlaid on the map were complex symbols, troop movement indicators, target icons pinpointing government buildings, communication hubs, key infrastructure, even specific individuals marked with ominous red Xs. Timelines ran along the bottom, indicating phased actions, escalating incidents. It wasn't just a map; it was a blueprint.

"My God," Elena breathed, stepping closer, her earlier search forgotten. "Look at this." She pointed to icons representing coordinated riots in major cities, targeted assassinations of political figures and journalists, sabotage of power grids, all timed to culminate in what looked like multiple, simultaneous coup attempts facilitated by paramilitary units – Jaguar's trainees, no doubt – inserted beforehand. "Operation 'Serpiente

Emplumada'. Plumed Serpent."

This was it. The destabilization plot Elena had suspected, laid out in chilling detail. The objective was clear: to shatter the existing governments, create a power vacuum, likely allowing Zukhov's syndicate, or whoever they represented, to install puppet regimes favorable to their interests — narcotics trafficking, resource exploitation, arms dealing on a national scale. The stolen documents I was hired to retrieve suddenly felt insignificant compared to this. Or maybe they were connected? Maybe Ramirez had uncovered this plot, and that was the data hidden on the documents?

"We need to copy this," Elena said urgently, pulling a high-capacity flash drive from her pocket and trying to interface it with the mapping table's console. "This is proof, undeniable proof—"

Click.

The sound came from the hallway, loud in the quiet building. The distinct sound of the electronic lock on the corridor fire door disengaging. Footsteps followed, heavy, measured, coming towards the records office.

Elena froze, yanking her flash drive out. "Security sweep! They're early!"

We exchanged a look, the uneasy truce solidifying into shared, immediate peril. We had the intel, the horrifying scope of the syndicate's plan displayed on the screen in front of us, but we were deep inside the command center, and Jaguar's men were right outside the door. Escape route, blocked. Backs against the wall. The game had just changed again, and the odds were plummeting towards zero.

"Keycard!" Elena hissed, her eyes wide in the dim glow of the mapping table, the horrific scope of 'Operation Serpiente Emplumada' still burning on the screen. The soft electronic click from the hallway echoed like a gunshot. Footsteps halted right outside the records office door.

No time for finesse. As the door handle began to turn, I lunged, grabbing the data card from the reader slot, pocketing it instinctively. Simultaneously, I shoved the heavy base of the mapping table console with all my strength. It wasn't graceful, but the multi-million dollar piece of hardware tipped, crashing against the inward-opening door with a sickening crunch of metal and composite materials just as two khaki-clad mercs started to enter.

The impact knocked them back, creating a momentary logjam, shouts of surprise turning instantly to rage. Elena didn't hesitate. Her suppressed pistol spat twice, aiming low through the gap, eliciting pained grunts. "The window!" she yelled, already moving towards the room's single, reinforced window overlooking the dark compound. It wasn't designed to be opened.

"No time!" I yelled back, seeing more figures crowding the hallway behind the first two. Alarms suddenly shrieked throughout the building, triggered by the commotion or the door breach attempt. Red emergency strobes kicked in, bathing the corridor in frantic pulses of light. "Diversion!" I grabbed a heavy workstation monitor, ripped its cords free, and hurled it into the bank of humming servers along the wall. Sparks erupted, screens went black, and a rank electrical burning smell filled the air. Smoke detectors shrieked, adding to the cacophony.

Using the chaos, I fired two shots towards the jammed doorway, forcing the mercs back momentarily, then sprinted towards Elena. She hadn't wasted time arguing; she'd used the butt of her pistol to star the reinforced windowpane near the latch mechanism. "Together!" she yelled over the din. We slammed our shoulders against the weakened glass just as bullets ripped through the office door from the hallway.

The window gave way with a screech of tortured metal and shattering polymer, dumping us unceremoniously onto the damp grass outside, about ten feet below. I landed badly, jarring my already aching bones, the impact stealing my breath. Elena rolled, coming up instantly, pistol scanning the darkness.

Lights snapped on around the compound, guards converging towards the administration building, drawn by the alarms and gunfire. Figures ran across the manicured lawns, beams from weapon-mounted lights cutting through the night. We were exposed, momentarily blinded.

"This way! Move!" Elena grabbed my arm, hauling me up, pulling me towards the deeper shadows where the curated landscaping met the untamed jungle. We plunged into the treeline just as automatic fire erupted behind us, chewing up the ground where we'd landed.

Running through the jungle at night, hunted, was a special kind of hell. Branches whipped at our faces, unseen roots threatened to trip us at every step, the thick, humid air burned in our lungs. Behind us, we could hear shouts, the crashing sounds of pursuit, the occasional snap of a twig too close for comfort. They had night vision; we had darkness and Elena's knowledge of the terrain near the west wing.

"They'll circle around," she panted, pulling me down a steep, muddy embankment towards a shallow stream. "Head for the old research station perimeter breach! It's our only way out!"

We splashed through the stream, the cool water a brief shock against overheated skin, then scrambled up the opposite bank, mud sucking at our boots. We ran, adrenaline masking the aches and the growing exhaustion, driven by the primal need to escape the closing net. We heard them flanking us now, moving through the jungle to our left and right, trying to herd us.

A burst of suppressed gunfire zipped through the leaves just ahead. A probe. They were guessing our path. We veered sharply right, deeper into a tangled section thick with vines and thorns that tore at our clothes. Progress slowed to a crawl, the sounds of pursuit falling slightly behind, but the tension remained wound tight.

An hour later, scratched, bruised, soaked in sweat and muddy water, we finally reached the gully where I'd entered the reserve. It seemed like a lifetime ago. The Land Cruiser had to be close. We paused in the relative safety of the gully's deep shadows, gasping for breath, listening. The main pursuit seemed to have fallen back, maybe regrouping, maybe assuming we were still heading deeper into the reserve. For the moment, we were clear.

Elena turned to me, her face pale and strained in the darkness, her eyes glittering with anger. "Alright, Callahan. You got us out. Now, Ramirez's data. Did you find anything in there? Anything he hid?"

I shook my head, still breathing hard, clutching the data card in my pocket. The card containing the blueprint for Operation Serpiente Emplumada. "Nothing specific on Ramirez's personal research. Place was mostly Jaguar's command post. But I found this." I decided partial honesty was required, though the instinct to trust her was completely gone now. "Operational plans. Big ones. Looks like a coordinated destabilization plot targeting half of Central America."

## CHAPTER 4

Her eyes narrowed. "Let me see it."

"No."

"What do you mean, 'no'?" Her voice was dangerously low. "We got that together. That intel belongs to both of us. My agency needs to see it."

"Your agency?" I countered. "The one that has you posing as a biologist while a paramilitary army trains next door? Who are you really working for, Elena?" I still didn't know her true affiliation, only that she opposed Jaguar, maybe.

"That doesn't matter right now!" she snapped. "What matters is that data could stop whatever Jaguar is planning! And it might contain clues about Ramirez! Give it to me, Callahan!"

"My client hired me to retrieve documents," I lied, falling back on my cover story. "This data card might contain those documents, or leads to them. It's what I'm getting paid for. It leaves with me." The half-million payday suddenly felt very distant, replaced by the chilling weight of the conspiracy outlined on that card. This was bigger than my contract. Bigger than Ramirez. Bigger, maybe, than Zukhov.

"Your client?" Her laugh was harsh, bitter. "Who sends one man into a place like this? Unless your client knew what was here? Knew about Serpiente Emplumada? Maybe they just wanted confirmation, or wanted the plans for themselves! Maybe you're working for the people who killed Mateo!"

The accusation hung in the air between us, ugly and venomous. The fragile trust, born of shared danger, shattered completely. She saw me as a mercenary, maybe even complicit. I saw her as an unknown quantity, potentially compromised, her focus dangerously narrow.

"I'm getting this intel out," I said flatly. "What you do is your business."

"And Ramirez? His research? You're just abandoning that?"

"Someone else will find it if it's meant to be found," I said, turning towards the direction of the hidden Land Cruiser. "Right now, stopping coups and potential massacres seems like the bigger priority. You disagree?"

She stared at me, her expression a mixture of fury and disillusionment. "I knew I shouldn't have trusted you. You're just like them. Using people, discarding them."

"Maybe," I said, not looking back. "But I'm still alive. Keep your head down, Elena."

I pushed through the last bit of jungle, found the Land Cruiser undisturbed. Starting the engine felt like triggering a beacon, but there was no choice. I had to get clear. As I bumped the truck back onto the overgrown spur road, I glanced in the rearview mirror. No sign of Elena. She had melted back into the jungle, alone, distrustful, maybe heading back towards the hornet's nest to pursue her own agenda.

I gunned the engine, splashing through the mud, leaving Santuario Verde and its deadly secrets behind me. I had the data card. I had the horrifying knowledge of Operation Serpiente Emplumada. But I was alone again, driving through the Costa Rican darkness, with a broken alliance behind me and Jaguar's hunters likely not far behind. The jungle had been escaped, but the tide of deception was pulling me deeper still.

## Chapter 5

"Ready?" Elena whispered, her voice barely audible above the drone of insects outside. We were crouched by a low maintenance hatch set into the rear wall of the administration building, concealed by thick, flowering bushes that filled the night air with a cloying sweetness. The harsh security lights didn't quite penetrate this deep into the decorative planting.

"As I'll ever be," I murmured back, scanning the shadows one last time. "You're sure about this hatch? Looks like it hasn't been opened since Cortez."

"It bypasses the main door sensors and the pressure plates in the immediate entryway. Leads to a utility crawlspace adjacent to the west wing offices. Ramirez showed it to me once, said it was an emergency egress from the old generator room before they built this monstrosity." She produced a thin, specialized tool. "Standard magnetic lock, easily overridden if you know how." She inserted the tool, manipulated it briefly, and the hatch clicked open with unnerving loudness in the relative quiet.

"After you," I gestured. No point arguing chivalry when dealing with potential booby traps or waiting guards.

She gave me a look that could curdle milk but slid silently through the opening into the pitch blackness beyond. I followed, pulling the hatch closed behind us as gently as possible. The air inside was cool, stale, smelling of dust and ozone. We were in a narrow crawlspace, pipes and conduits lining the walls. Elena clicked on a penlight shielded with a red filter, casting an eerie, limited glow.

"Stay close," she breathed. "There are infrared beams in the main corridors, tied into the cameras. We need to reach the central records office – Ramirez kept hard copies of almost everything there, paranoid about digital failures. If his research notes exist anywhere, they'll be there."

We moved like ghosts through the building's hidden veins, Elena navigating by memory, me watching our backs, pistol ready, every creak of the structure, every hum of machinery setting my nerves on edge. Twice, we froze as heavy footsteps echoed from the corridor beyond the thin wall, waiting until they passed. It felt like crawling through the guts of some sleeping concrete beast.

Finally, Elena stopped, pointing her dim red light at a ventilation grille higher up on the crawlspace wall. "This looks into the records office hallway. Should be clear this time of night, but check."

I eased up, peered through the grille. A long, sterile corridor stretched left and right, lit by dim overhead emergency lights. Empty. "Clear."

Getting out of the crawlspace and into the office itself involved bypassing another electronic lock on a heavy fire door – Elena handled that with unnerving speed – and then disabling the office door's simpler magnetic lock and pressure sensor. We slipped inside, closing the door silently behind us.

The records office wasn't what I expected. Less dusty archives, more modern command hub. Banks of servers hummed quietly along one wall. Multiple workstations sat dark. Filing cabinets lined another wall, but they looked too standard for Ramirez's critical research. In the center of the room, a large digital mapping table, currently dark, dominated the space. This wasn't just where records were kept; this was where Jaguar, or someone high up, *worked.*

"Ramirez's specific project files wouldn't be out here," Elena whispered, moving towards a workstation. "He had a private safe, supposedly fireproof, somewhere in his main office down the hall. But maybe the access logs..." She began carefully working on the keyboard, using what looked like a sophisticated decryption device plugged into a USB port.

While she worked the digital angle, I did the physical sweep. Checked the filing cabinets – personnel files for the mercs (code-names mostly), training schedules, requisitions for ammunition and supplies – confirming the scale of the camp but nothing on Ramirez or the documents. No obvious safes. I moved towards the large mapping table. Its surface was dark, but a faint power light glowed on the console. Maybe it held recent operational data.

"Anything?" I asked Elena, keeping my voice low.

"Firewalls are serious," she muttered, frowning at the screen. "Military grade. Trying a backdoor exploit Ramirez mentioned once..."

I examined the mapping table console. No obvious power switch, likely controlled remotely or from a master terminal. But there was a small slot, like for a data card. And tucked slightly underneath, almost out of sight, was a slim black data card reader, still plugged in. Someone had forgotten, or been interrupted while using it. Beside it lay a single data card, looking innocuous. Curiosity, or maybe just a hunch born of desperation, made me pick it up. No label. I glanced at Elena, still engrossed in her decryption attempt. Slipping the card into the reader felt like a gamble, but sitting idle wasn't helping.

The large screen above the table flickered to life, startling both of us. Elena spun around, hand reaching for her weapon. "What did you do?"

"Found a data card," I said, pointing.

The screen resolved into a detailed topographical map, not of Costa Rica, but of the northern triangle of Central America – Guatemala, Honduras, El Salvador. Overlaid on the map were complex symbols, troop movement indicators, target icons pinpointing government buildings, communication hubs, key infrastructure, even specific individuals marked with ominous red Xs. Timelines ran along the bottom, indicating phased actions, escalating incidents. It wasn't just a map; it was a blueprint.

"My God," Elena breathed, stepping closer, her earlier search forgotten. "Look at this." She pointed to icons representing coordinated riots in major cities, targeted assassinations of political figures and journalists, sabotage of power grids, all timed to culminate in what looked like multiple, simultaneous coup attempts facilitated by paramilitary units – Jaguar's trainees, no doubt – inserted beforehand. "Operation 'Serpiente Emplumada'. Plumed Serpent."

This was it. The destabilization plot Elena had suspected, laid out in chilling detail. The objective was clear: to shatter the existing governments, create a power vacuum, likely allowing Zukhov's syndicate, or whoever they represented, to install puppet regimes favorable to their interests – narcotics trafficking, resource exploitation, arms dealing on a national scale. The stolen documents I was hired to retrieve suddenly felt insignificant compared to this. Or maybe they were connected?

## CHAPTER 5

Maybe Ramirez had uncovered this plot, and *that* was the data hidden on the documents?

"We need to copy this," Elena said urgently, pulling a high-capacity flash drive from her pocket and trying to interface it with the mapping table's console. "This is proof, undeniable proof—"

*Click.*

The sound came from the hallway, loud in the quiet building. The distinct sound of the electronic lock on the corridor fire door disengaging. Footsteps followed, heavy, measured, coming towards the records office.

Elena froze, yanking her flash drive out. "Security sweep! They're early!"

We exchanged a look, the uneasy truce solidifying into shared, immediate peril. We had the intel, the horrifying scope of the syndicate's plan displayed on the screen in front of us, but we were deep inside the command center, and Jaguar's men were right outside the door. Escape route, blocked. Backs against the wall. The game had just changed again, and the odds were plummeting towards zero.

## Chapter 6

"Keycard!" Elena hissed, her eyes wide in the dim glow of the mapping table, the horrific scope of 'Operation Serpiente Emplumada' still burning on the screen. The soft electronic click from the hallway echoed like a gunshot. Footsteps halted right outside the records office door.

No time for finesse. As the door handle began to turn, I lunged, grabbing the data card from the reader slot, pocketing it instinctively. Simultaneously, I shoved the heavy base of the mapping table console with all my strength. It wasn't graceful, but the multi-million dollar piece of hardware tipped, crashing against the inward-opening door with a sickening crunch of metal and composite materials just as two khaki-clad mercs started to enter.

The impact knocked them back, creating a momentary logjam, shouts of surprise turning instantly to rage. Elena didn't hesitate. Her suppressed pistol spat twice, aiming low through the gap, eliciting pained grunts. "The window!" she yelled, already moving towards the room's single, reinforced window overlooking the dark compound. It wasn't designed to be opened.

"No time!" I yelled back, seeing more figures crowding the hallway behind the first two. Alarms suddenly shrieked throughout the building, triggered by the commotion or the door breach attempt. Red emergency strobes kicked in, bathing the corridor in frantic pulses of light. "Diversion!" I grabbed a heavy workstation monitor, ripped its cords free, and hurled it into the bank of humming servers along the wall. Sparks erupted, screens went black, and a rank electrical burning smell filled the air. Smoke detectors shrieked, adding to the cacophony.

Using the chaos, I fired two shots towards the jammed doorway, forcing the mercs back momentarily, then sprinted towards Elena. She hadn't wasted time arguing; she'd used the butt of her pistol to star the reinforced windowpane near the latch mechanism. "Together!" she yelled over the din. We slammed our shoulders against the weakened glass just as bullets ripped through the office door from the hallway.

The window gave way with a screech of tortured metal and shattering polymer, dumping us unceremoniously onto the damp grass outside, about ten feet below. I landed badly, jarring my already aching bones, the impact stealing my breath. Elena rolled, coming up instantly, pistol scanning the darkness.

Lights snapped on around the compound, guards converging towards the administration building, drawn by the alarms and gunfire. Figures ran across the manicured lawns, beams from weapon-mounted lights cutting through the night. We were exposed, momentarily blinded.

"This way! Move!" Elena grabbed my arm, hauling me up, pulling me towards the deeper shadows where the curated landscaping met the untamed jungle. We plunged into the treeline just as automatic fire erupted behind us, chewing up the ground where we'd landed.

Running through the jungle at night, hunted, was a special kind of hell. Branches whipped at our faces, unseen roots threatened to trip us at every step, the thick, humid air burned in our lungs. Behind us, we could hear shouts, the crashing sounds of pursuit, the occasional snap of a twig too close for comfort. They had night vision; we had darkness and Elena's knowledge of the terrain near the west wing.

"They'll circle around," she panted, pulling me down a steep, muddy embankment towards a shallow stream. "Head for the old research station perimeter breach! It's our only way out!"

We splashed through the stream, the cool water a brief shock against overheated skin, then scrambled up the opposite bank, mud sucking at our boots. We ran, adrenaline masking the aches and the growing exhaustion, driven by the primal need to escape the closing net. We heard them flanking us now, moving through the jungle to our left and right, trying to herd us.

A burst of suppressed gunfire zipped through the leaves just ahead. A probe. They were guessing our path. We veered sharply right, deeper into a tangled section thick with vines and thorns that tore at our clothes. Progress slowed to a crawl, the sounds of pursuit falling slightly behind, but the tension remained wound tight.

An hour later, scratched, bruised, soaked in sweat and muddy water, we finally reached the gully where I'd entered the reserve. It seemed like a lifetime ago. The Land Cruiser had to be close. We paused in the relative safety of the gully's deep shadows, gasping for breath, listening. The main pursuit seemed to have fallen back, maybe regrouping, maybe assuming we were still heading deeper into the reserve. For the moment, we were clear.

Elena turned to me, her face pale and strained in the darkness, her eyes glittering with anger. "Alright, Callahan. You got us out. Now, Ramirez's data. Did you find anything in there? Anything he hid?"

I shook my head, still breathing hard, clutching the data card in my pocket. The card containing the blueprint for Operation Serpiente Emplumada. "Nothing specific on Ramirez's personal research. Place was mostly Jaguar's command post. But I found *this*." I decided partial honesty was required, though the instinct to trust her was completely gone now. "Operational plans. Big ones. Looks like a coordinated destabilization plot targeting half of Central America."

Her eyes narrowed. "Let me see it."

"No."

"What do you mean, 'no'?" Her voice was dangerously low. "We got that together. That intel belongs to both of us. My agency needs to see it."

"Your agency?" I countered. "The one that has you posing as a biologist while a paramilitary army trains next door? Who are you really working for, Elena?" I still didn't know her true affiliation, only that she opposed Jaguar, maybe.

"That doesn't matter right now!" she snapped. "What matters is that data could stop whatever Jaguar is planning! And it might contain clues about Ramirez! Give it to me, Callahan!"

"My client hired me to retrieve documents," I lied, falling back on my cover story. "This data card might contain those documents, or leads to them. It's what I'm getting paid for. It leaves with me." The half-million payday suddenly felt very distant, replaced by the chilling weight of the conspiracy outlined on that card. This was bigger than my contract. Bigger than Ramirez. Bigger, maybe, than Zukhov.

"Your client?" Her laugh was harsh, bitter. "Who sends one man into a place like this? Unless your client *knew* what was here? Knew about Serpiente Emplumada? Maybe they just wanted confirmation, or wanted the plans for themselves!

Maybe you're working for the people who *killed* Mateo!"

The accusation hung in the air between us, ugly and venomous. The fragile trust, born of shared danger, shattered completely. She saw me as a mercenary, maybe even complicit. I saw her as an unknown quantity, potentially compromised, her focus dangerously narrow.

"I'm getting this intel out," I said flatly. "What you do is your business."

"And Ramirez? His research? You're just abandoning that?"

"Someone else will find it if it's meant to be found," I said, turning towards the direction of the hidden Land Cruiser. "Right now, stopping coups and potential massacres seems like the bigger priority. You disagree?"

She stared at me, her expression a mixture of fury and disillusionment. "I knew I shouldn't have trusted you. You're just like them. Using people, discarding them."

"Maybe," I said, not looking back. "But I'm still alive. Keep your head down, Elena."

I pushed through the last bit of jungle, found the Land Cruiser undisturbed. Starting the engine felt like triggering a beacon, but there was no choice. I had to get clear. As I bumped the truck back onto the overgrown spur road, I glanced in the rearview mirror. No sign of Elena. She had melted back into the jungle, alone, distrustful, maybe heading back towards the hornet's nest to pursue her own agenda.

I gunned the engine, splashing through the mud, leaving Santuario Verde and its deadly secrets behind me. I had the data card. I had the horrifying knowledge of Operation Serpiente Emplumada. But I was alone again, driving through the Costa Rican darkness, with a broken alliance behind me and Jaguar's hunters likely not far behind. The jungle had been escaped, but

## CHAPTER 6

the tide of deception was pulling me deeper still.

# Chapter 7

The Land Cruiser bucked and slewed through the muddy ruts, engine whining in protest, headlights cutting a swathe through the suffocating darkness of the Osa Peninsula night. Behind me lay Santuario Verde, a hornet's nest I'd kicked over, its guards now swarming, undoubtedly coordinating a search. Ahead lay... uncertainty. And the long, treacherous drive back towards something resembling civilization. I gripped the wheel, knuckles white, every nerve endings still humming from the escape, the firefight, the bitter parting with Elena. The data card containing the Serpiente Emplumada plans felt like a physical weight in my pocket. Proof of a conspiracy that could ignite Central America, entrusted to a fugitive driving a stolen rental through hostile territory. Smart money would have been on me not making it till dawn.

Rain started, not a gentle shower, but a tropical downpour, thick sheets of water slamming against the windshield, instantly turning the already treacherous track into a river of slick mud. The wipers struggled, smearing grime across the glass. Visibility dropped to near zero. Perfect conditions for an ambush. Or an accident.

It came in the form of a massive Ceiba tree, probably weakened by the rain-soaked earth, choosing that exact moment to collapse across the track maybe fifty yards ahead. One second I was wrestling the wheel through a muddy slide, the next my headlights illuminated an impenetrable wall of thick trunk and tangled branches completely blocking the path. I slammed on the brakes, skidding to a halt just feet from the unexpected roadblock. Engine stalled. Silence, except for the deafening roar of rain on the roof and the frantic thumping of my own heart.

Dead end. No way forward in the vehicle. Backtracking towards the hornet's nest was suicide. Which left pushing into the jungle on foot. I killed the headlights, grabbed my pack and pistol, and was just about to ease the door open when a voice spoke, calm and quiet, from the dripping darkness just outside my window.

"Going somewhere, Mr. Kincaid? Or should I call you Callahan?"

I froze, pistol instinctively coming up, pointing towards the unseen speaker. Rain streamed down the window, distorting everything outside into a watery nightmare. A shadow detached itself from the deeper gloom near the fallen tree, coalescing into the shape of a man. Tall, lean, dressed in dark, practical rain gear, he moved with an unnerving lack of sound despite the downpour. He held a suppressed pistol, aimed casually but expertly at my head through the glass. His face, briefly illuminated as he moved, was sharp, angular, with pale eyes that seemed to absorb the minimal light. European, maybe Scandinavian. Definitely professional. Definitely not one of Jaguar's grunts.

"Depends who's asking," I replied, my voice tight, keeping my own weapon steady.

"Let's call me Lars," the man said. His English was precise, barely accented. "And I'm asking for the data card you removed from the Santuario Verde administration building approximately ninety minutes ago. The one containing the details of Operation Serpiente Emplumada."

My blood ran cold. He knew my name – or one of them. He knew about the card, knew its contents. He wasn't guessing. "Seems you're well informed, Lars."

"My employers make it their business to be informed. They have a vested interest in ensuring Operation Serpiente Emplumada does not succeed. That data card is crucial." He took a step closer, rain dripping from the brim of his waterproof hat. "Hand it over, Mr. Kincaid, and perhaps you walk away from this."

"Your employers," I repeated. "Friends of Zukhov? Or competitors?"

A faint smile touched Lars's lips, gone as quickly as it appeared. "Let's just say we represent... dissenting shareholders within the broader enterprise. Zukhov and Jaguar's current project is considered reckless, destabilizing in ways counterproductive to long-term profitability." He gestured with his pistol. "The card, please. No sudden movements."

So, a rival faction. Trying to sabotage Zukhov's operation from within, or perhaps take it over. And they'd sent Lars to retrieve the proof, the blueprint. Was he the one watching me in Puerto Jiménez? Was he the one who shot Mateo?

"Tell me, Lars," I asked, stalling, my eyes scanning the jungle edges behind him, listening over the rain. "Was it you who retired my contact back in town? Efficient work."

"The local man? Irrelevant," Lars dismissed coolly. "He served his purpose by confirming your arrival. My priority was securing the data once you retrieved it. Less complicated than infiltrating Jaguar's little fortress myself. You did the hard part." He sounded almost appreciative. "Now, the card."

Before I could formulate another delaying tactic, Lars's head snapped up, his gaze shifting towards the track behind my stalled Land Cruiser. His body tensed. I heard it too, then – faint at first over the rain, but growing rapidly louder – the strained whine of approaching vehicle engines, plural. Headlight beams, diffused by the downpour, cut weakly through the trees.

Jaguar's pursuit. They hadn't given up. They were tracking the Land Cruiser.

Lars cursed under his breath, a sharp, sibilant sound. His pale eyes met mine through the rain-streaked window. The calculation was instant, pragmatic. "Jaguar's apes. They arrive in two minutes, maybe less. They find us here, they kill us both. No questions, no discussion of corporate dissent."

He lowered his pistol slightly, though not entirely away from me. "New proposal, Kincaid. Temporary alliance. We deal with the immediate threat. Get clear of this track, lose them in the jungle. Afterwards," his faint smile returned, "we can revisit the ownership of the data card. Agreed?"

Trapped between a professional killer who wanted my intel and a paramilitary kill squad that wanted me dead. Some choice. "Agreed," I gritted out. "For now."

"Excellent." Lars moved fast, gesturing towards the passenger side. "Out. Grab your gear. We go on foot. Now!"

I shoved my door open, grabbing my pack, pistol ready. Lars was already melting into the jungle on the opposite side of the track. Headlights were closer now, maybe half a mile back, bouncing wildly on the rough terrain.

We plunged into the undergrowth, the jungle swallowing us instantly. Lars moved with incredible speed and silence, clearly equipped with night vision, forcing me to push hard just to keep up, relying on instinct and the faint ambient light filtering through the canopy. Behind us, we heard the pursuit vehicles skid to a halt near the fallen tree and my abandoned Land Cruiser. Shouted commands, flashlight beams stabbing erratically into the jungle.

"This way," Lars hissed, changing direction, leading us towards the sound of rushing water. A river, maybe?

We broke through onto the muddy bank of a rain-swollen river, wider and faster than the streams I'd crossed earlier. Dangerous in the dark. On the far bank, maybe thirty yards across the churning brown water, the jungle looked equally dense, impenetrable.

Just as we reached the bank, figures burst from the treeline behind us, flashlights pinning us. "There! Hold it!"

Gunfire erupted, suppressed cracks muffled by the rain, bullets kicking up mud and water around us. Lars didn't hesitate. He returned fire with clinical precision – two shots, two figures dropping – then grabbed my arm. "Move! Into the water!"

We scrambled down the bank, plunging into the surprisingly cold, fast-moving river. The current immediately grabbed at my legs, threatening to sweep me away. Lars was already striking out for the far bank, swimming powerfully. Behind us, more shots, the beams of flashlights playing frantically over the water's surface.

We clawed our way onto the opposite bank, soaked, gasping, melting back into the jungle's embrace just as the lights found the spot where we'd emerged. We pushed deeper, putting distance between us and the river, the sounds of pursuit hopefully masked by the roar of the water and the continuing downpour.

Finally, miles later it felt like, Lars signaled a halt in a slightly sheltered spot beneath a tangle of thick roots. We crouched in the darkness, listening. Only the sound of the rain dripping through the leaves. We'd lost them, for now.

We were alive. Temporary allies. Each of us possessing something the other wanted. Each of us knowing the truce would only last as long as the immediate threat from Jaguar remained. Lars looked at me, his pale eyes unreadable in the gloom. The deadly bargain had been struck. Survival first. Betrayal, undoubtedly, would come later.

## Chapter 8

We moved through the pre-dawn jungle like wraiths, pushed by adrenaline and the fear of pursuit, the only sounds our own ragged breathing and the constant drip of water from the saturated canopy overhead. The rain had eased to a drizzle, but the ground underfoot was a treacherous soup of mud and decaying vegetation. Lars, despite the conditions, moved with an unnerving, predatory grace, his pale eyes constantly scanning, missing nothing. The uneasy truce held, enforced by the shared threat somewhere behind us in the darkness. We didn't speak, conserving energy, each lost in his own calculations.

Just as the first grey hint of dawn began to filter through the impossibly thick leaves, Lars signaled a halt. He'd found it – a shallow rock overhang, barely a cave, hidden behind a curtain of vines near a small, moss-choked waterfall. Not comfortable, not dry, but defensible and, most importantly, concealed.

"We rest here," he stated, his voice flat, devoid of warmth. He slipped off his pack, produced a compact scanner, and did a quick sweep for electronic surveillance. Finding none, he nodded curtly. "Clear for now. They'll widen their search pattern at daylight, maybe use dogs if Jaguar is truly irritated. We need to know exactly what is on that card before we move again."

He pulled a ruggedized tablet from his pack, along with a

universal card reader attachment. He looked at me expectantly, holding out his hand.

Every instinct screamed not to trust him, not to give him access to the only piece of leverage I had. But he was right. Deep in the jungle, wounded (though I hid the extent of the aches and the gash on my arm), low on supplies, I needed to know what I was carrying. And his gear was likely better encrypted, harder to trace if we accessed sensitive files, than anything I had left after ditching my laptop back in Florida. Reluctantly, I fished the tiny data card from the waterproof pouch where I'd secured it. I didn't hand it to him.

"You run the reader. I insert the card. We both watch the screen," I said. My pistol rested casually on my knee, pointed vaguely in his direction.

Lars gave that faint, cold smile again. "Pragmatic. I approve." He set up the tablet, plugged in the reader. I carefully inserted Varga's chip.

The file structure that popped up was chaotic, nested, some files clearly encrypted, others seemingly mundane sanctuary research notes – Varga's or Ramirez's digital camouflage. Lars's fingers moved quickly across the virtual keyboard, running decryption algorithms, bypassing simple password protections.

"She was clever," he admitted grudgingly. "Layered encryption, some older military protocols, mixed with standard commercial stuff. Trying to hide the important data within the noise."

First, the 'Serpiente Emplumada' files opened, confirming what we'd glimpsed on the mapping table. Detailed plans, phases laid out with chilling military precision. Target lists that included specific names – politicians, generals, journalists across three Central American nations. Logistics routes, weapon caches (beyond the Everglades one?), communication protocols. It was staggering in its audacity, its scope. Enough to burn the region down.

"My employers were correct," Lars murmured, scrolling through the target lists. "Zukhov is overreaching. This level of chaos benefits no one in the long run."

"Except Zukhov," I countered. "And whoever is footing the bill."

"Precisely," Lars agreed. "Which brings us to the funding." He navigated away from the operational plans, digging deeper into encrypted financial folders Varga must have copied or intercepted. Spreadsheets, wire transfer records disguised as grant disbursements or investment flows, communications referencing account numbers routed through Panama, Liechtenstein, the Caymans. Standard syndicate bookkeeping, designed to be impenetrable.

"Can you crack those account names? Trace the source?" I asked.

Lars frowned, running another program. "Difficult. Heavy encryption, anonymized routing. But Varga left... fragments. Metadata tags. Partially deleted routing headers within coded emails between Jaguar and someone designated only as 'Alpha'. She must have been trying to piece it together herself." He worked silently for several minutes, the only sound the dripping water outside and the soft tapping on the screen. Then he stopped. "Got it. Cross-referenced the partial account numbers and routing protocols with known high-level syndicate financial activity my employers monitor. One name keeps appearing, linked directly to the authorization codes for Serpiente Emplumada's primary funding disbursements."

He turned the tablet slightly so I could see the screen. A name displayed below a string of secure account numbers and cryptic authorization codes: **VANCE, SILAS.** Followed by a Panama City corporate address for 'Vance Global Holdings'.

Silas Vance. The name echoed Silas Thorne, another untouchable pillar of respectable wealth I'd encountered back in Florida. Coincidence? Or was there a type? Vance Global Holdings... the name rang a faint bell, something connected to international shipping or commodity trading, enormous, discreet, powerful. He wasn't just a financier; he was the financier for this operation. Maybe higher up the food chain than Croft? The mastermind, just as the outline hinted. Panama. Where dirty money flowed like water through the Canal.

"Silas Vance," I said aloud. "He's Alpha? He's funding this whole war?"

"It appears so," Lars confirmed, his expression unreadable. "He controls the purse strings for Jaguar, and likely Zukhov's Central American expansion. Neutralizing Vance would likely cripple Operation Serpiente Emplumada." He looked at me, his pale eyes locking onto mine. "Which is precisely what my employers intend to do. The data card, Kincaid. It contains the proof needed."

The fragile truce, already strained, snapped. The immediate threat from Jaguar's men seemed, for the moment, less pressing than the cold-blooded professional sitting across from me.

"Your employers can get their own proof, Lars," I said, carefully ejecting the data card and pocketing it. "This stays with me."

"That was not our agreement," Lars said, his voice dangerously soft. "The agreement was survival first. We have survived the first wave. Now, the card." His hand rested near the grip of his pistol.

"The agreement was temporary," I shot back. "I don't work for your 'employers'. I don't know their agenda. Maybe they just want to replace Zukhov and Vance, run the show themselves. This intel doesn't belong to them."

"And you think it belongs to you? Or your mysterious, anonymous client?" Lars scoffed. "You are a mercenary, Kincaid. A tool. Don't delude yourself."

"Maybe," I conceded. "But right now, I'm the tool holding the blueprints. And I'm not handing them over." We stared at each other, the tension thick enough to choke on. A fight here, now, would be stupid, maybe fatal for both of us, and would likely bring Jaguar's men running. We both knew it.

Lars finally broke the silence, a thin smile touching his lips again. "Very well. Keep it. For now. But understand this: my mission is to acquire that data. My employers are patient, but persistent. We will have it, Kincaid. One way or another." He began packing his gear with swift efficiency. "I suggest you find your way out of Costa Rica quickly. Jaguar will be turning this peninsula inside out looking for you. And now Vance knows his operation is compromised."

"Where are you going?"

"Panama, eventually," Lars said, shouldering his pack. "To observe Mr. Vance. And perhaps... create opportunities. Unlike you, I have resources, support." He paused at the edge of the overhang, looking back at me. "Stay out of my way, Kincaid. Next time, the truce is off."

Then he was gone, vanishing silently back into the rain-soaked jungle, leaving me alone in the damp, cramped shelter. Alone with the knowledge of Silas Vance, the Panama connection, the imminent threat of Operation Serpiente Emplumada, and the certainty that I now had at least three sets of deadly pro-

## CHAPTER 8

fessionals hunting me – Jaguar's mercs, Lars's shadowy faction, and whoever the hell hired me in the first place. Surviving the jungle was just the first step. Getting to Panama and dealing with Vance... that was a whole new storm brewing.

# Chapter 9

Getting out of the Costa Rican jungle was a slow, miserable, nerve-shredding affair. It involved days of careful trekking, avoiding known routes, leveraging local knowledge gleaned from Mateo's brief warnings, and ultimately paying an exorbitant sum to a dubious character running illicit speedboat charters out of a hidden cove, destination anywhere but Costa Rica. I landed on a nameless stretch of beach on Panama's northern coast two days later, looking like something the tide had washed in and decided it didn't want. From there, it was buses, borrowed clothes, and fabricated travel papers – courtesy of the last alias Sully had provided – to make my way south to the gleaming, humid, money-soaked metropolis of Panama City.

The contrast with the Osa Peninsula was jarring. Gone was the suffocating green, replaced by towering glass and steel scraping the sky, the relentless thrum of commerce, the blare of horns in perpetual traffic jams, and the thick, wet heat radiating off concrete and asphalt. This city felt like Miami's slicker, more ruthless international cousin, built on canal fees and banking secrecy. A place where fortunes were made and laundered with equal efficiency, where men like Silas Vance could thrive,

## CHAPTER 9

hidden in plain sight behind layers of corporate respectability and philanthropic gloss.

Finding Vance wasn't hard; finding a way to him, that was the challenge. Vance Global Holdings occupied the top floors of one of the city's most prestigious waterfront towers, a fortress of smoked glass and private security. Initial reconnaissance, conducted carefully from crowded plazas and anonymous internet cafes using heavily encrypted connections, painted a picture of a man insulated by wealth and power. His schedule was managed by layers of assistants, his movements shielded by bodyguards who looked like they chewed nails for breakfast. But Vance, like Croft back in Florida, understood the value of public image. He cultivated connections, attended the right events.

And according to the society pages and financial news feeds I monitored, the 'right event' this week was the annual Pan-American Trade Gala, a lavish affair hosted at the restored ruins of a colonial-era convent in the heart of Casco Viejo, the city's historic old town. Ostensibly about promoting hemispheric trade, it was really a playground for the powerful – politicians, diplomats, financiers, industrialists – to schmooze, posture, and cut deals in chandelier-lit rooms. Vance was listed as a patron and keynote speaker. It was my best chance to get eyes on him, identify key associates, maybe plant a bug, or find an opening.

Getting into the Gala required finesse. My 'Thomas Callahan' photographer ID was useless here. I needed something better. A few discreet, encrypted messages back and forth with Sully, leveraging old contacts and favors owed, produced a minor miracle: credentials identifying me as 'Mr. David Rousseau,' an aide attached to the delegation from the Belgian trade commission – a delegation large enough, and obscure enough, that one extra vaguely European-looking face might just slip through unnoticed, especially if he kept his mouth shut and lingered near the canapés. Sully also provided schematics for the convent venue, highlighting security blind spots and potential access points.

Dressed in a borrowed suit that felt only slightly less uncomfortable than crawling through jungle mud, I arrived via taxi, blending into the stream of limousines and diplomatic vehicles disgorging guests in glittering gowns and tailored tuxedos. Security was tight – uniformed police, private guards, and watchful men in dark suits with coiled earpieces – but my Belgian credentials, cross-referenced against Sully's doctored list, got me through the door with only a cursory glance.

Inside, the air hummed with forced laughter, competing perfumes, and the murmur of a dozen languages. Waiters circulated with trays of champagne and tiny, exquisite bites of food. The restored convent was stunning – ancient stone walls juxtaposed with modern glass and steel, courtyards lit by flickering torches, the main hall echoing under vaulted ceilings. It was a world away from Santuario Verde's brutal functionality, but the underlying current of danger felt disturbingly similar. These people wielded power that could crush nations just as effectively as Jaguar's mercenaries, just with cleaner hands.

I spotted Silas Vance holding court near a massive baroque fountain in the main courtyard. He fit the part perfectly. Tall, silver-haired, tanned, radiating effortless charisma and absolute confidence. He laughed easily, shaking hands, gesturing animatedly, surrounded by deferential aides and attentive listeners – politicians, bankers, a striking woman dripping in emeralds who looked vaguely familiar (maybe from the Zukhov auction intel?). But his eyes, when they swept the crowd, were cold, sharp, missing nothing. Like a shark patrolling a coral reef. Observing him, I felt a chill despite the humid night air. This was the man funding Operation Serpiente Emplumada.

My plan was simple: get close, try to overhear conversations, maybe swap his drink coaster for one embedded with a micro-recorder during a moment of distraction. I drifted closer, pretending to admire the fountain, nursing a glass of champagne I didn't drink. Vance was talking about sustainable development initiatives, his voice smooth, persuasive. The hypocrisy was breathtaking.

As I edged nearer, trying to look like just another anonymous Euro-aide, one of Vance's bodyguards – a bull-necked man whose suit couldn't quite conceal the hardware underneath – turned his head slightly, his eyes locking onto mine. There was no flicker of recognition, just cold, professional assessment. He didn't like what he saw. Maybe I lingered too long. Maybe my suit wasn't quite right. Maybe my face, scanned by some discreet camera and run through a database, didn't perfectly match the blurry photo attached to 'David Rousseau's' file.

The bodyguard murmured something into his wrist-comm, his eyes never leaving mine. He started moving towards me, subtly but deliberately cutting off my path back towards the main hall. Another plainclothes security man detached himself from the edge of the crowd, angling to intercept me from the other side. The net was closing, quietly, efficiently. My cover was blown.

No time for subtlety now. I set the champagne flute down on the fountain's edge, turned, and walked briskly – not running, not yet – back towards the arched exit leading from the courtyard into the convent's labyrinthine interior. The bodyguards quickened their pace, no longer trying to be discreet.

I broke into a run, dodging startled guests, plunging through the archway into a dimly lit corridor lined with antique tapestries. Behind me, shouts, the sound of running feet. Ahead, the corridor branched. Left led back towards the main entrance and certain capture. Right led deeper into the old building, towards the service areas shown on Sully's schematics. I went right.

The pursuit was immediate, professional. They knew the layout. I slammed through a heavy wooden door marked 'Staff Only', finding myself in a narrow service hallway smelling of disinfectant and stale food. Another guard appeared at the far end, blocking my path. I fired my silenced pistol – still carrying it from Costa Rica, a risky necessity – twice, hitting him center mass. He went down without a sound, but the impact alerted the others.

I sprinted past him, down a flight of stone steps into what felt like ancient cellars, now used for storage. Barrels, crates, dusty furniture under white sheets. Multiple exits, but which one led out? I chose one at random, bursting out into a narrow, cobblestone alleyway behind the convent. Part of Casco Viejo. Tall, crumbling colonial buildings leaned overhead, balconies dripping laundry and bougainvillea. Freedom?

Not yet. Headlights flared at one end of the alley as a black SUV slewed around the corner, blocking the exit. Doors opened, men piling out. I spun, ran the other way, only to see another SUV blocking the far end. Pinned.

Up. Only way out was up. I spotted a rusty fire escape ladder bolted to the side of an adjacent building, leading towards the rooftops. I leaped, grabbed the lowest rung, and started climbing, my muscles screaming in protest, the wounds from the yacht and the jungle escape making themselves known again.

## CHAPTER 9

Below, shouts, then the crack of unsilenced gunfire, bullets sparking off the stone walls around me. They weren't worried about noise anymore.

Reaching the rooftop, I scrambled across terracotta tiles, heading towards the denser cluster of buildings deeper in the Old Town. Sirens wailed in the distance now, adding to the chaos. I glanced back. Figures were already emerging onto the rooftop behind me, fanning out. Vance's people were relentless.

I jumped across a narrow gap to the next rooftop, landed awkwardly, stumbled, but kept moving. Panama City sprawled around me, a glittering panorama of lights and shadows, utterly indifferent to the desperate chase unfolding across its historic heart. I had escaped the gala, but Vance knew I was here. I was exposed, hunted, alone in a city built on secrets and suspicion. Finding temporary refuge was easy; finding a way to strike back at Silas Vance had just become infinitely harder.

# Chapter 10

The room smelled of mildew, stale cigarette smoke, and desperation. It was a ten-dollar-a-night flop in El Chorrillo, a rough neighborhood bordering Casco Viejo, where questions weren't asked as long as the cash was good. Good enough wasn't the word; it was the last of my Costa Rica escape fund. I sat on the lumpy mattress, the single bare bulb overhead casting harsh shadows, the data card containing the blueprint for Operation Serpiente Emplumada plugged into the cheap, untraceable burner tablet I'd acquired. The timeline projected on the cracked screen was chillingly clear. Phase One – coordinated riots and assassinations – was already subtly underway according to encrypted chatter fragments Varga had captured. Phase Two – the paramilitary strikes, the coup attempts – was scheduled to activate within the next twelve hours. Go-signal pending final authorization from 'Alpha' – Silas Vance.

Vance knew I was here now. He'd sicced his dogs on me at the gala. Security would be tripled. His network would be on high alert. Getting near him again was impossible. Stopping the operation meant hitting its nerve center, the command hub coordinating Jaguar's teams in the field. But where was it? The data card showed encrypted communication nodes, but pinpointing the physical source...

## CHAPTER 10

A soft knock at the flimsy door. Not the landlord. Too quiet, too deliberate. I moved silently, pistol in hand, flattening myself against the wall beside the doorframe. "Who is it?" I kept my voice low, rough.

"Someone who doesn't want Central America to turn into a slaughterhouse tomorrow morning, Callahan." Elena's voice, muffled but unmistakable.

My surprise warred with deep suspicion. I cracked the door, chain still on, pistol held ready. She stood in the dim, humid hallway, looking as worn and wired as I felt, dressed in practical dark clothes, a small pack slung over her shoulder. No obvious weapon drawn, but I didn't doubt she was armed.

"How did you find me?" I asked, keeping the door chained.

"You're not as invisible as you think. Especially when half the private security in Casco Viejo is suddenly looking for a 'disruptive foreign guest'. I made an educated guess where someone needing to disappear might end up." Her eyes flicked past me, taking in the dismal room. "Nice place."

"It's got atmosphere. What do you want, Elena? Round two of 'who gets the data card'?"

"No," she said, her gaze intense, meeting mine directly. "I want to stop Serpiente Emplumada. Now. Before it's too late. Vance knows you saw the plans. He knows the operation is potentially compromised. Logic dictates he'll either accelerate the timeline or initiate it immediately before we can act."

She was right. The gala incident had forced Vance's hand. The 'go' signal wasn't just pending; it was likely imminent. "And you think we can stop it? Just the two of us?"

"We have the data," she countered. "And I've been doing my own digging since I got to Panama two days ago, trying to trace the command structure back from Jaguar. I think

I know where they're running the coordination hub." She held up her own burner tablet, displaying a satellite image overlaid with data. "This building. Listed as 'PanIsthmus Global Logistics' – a known Vance subsidiary near the Canal Zone. High-security communications array on the roof, unusual power consumption spikes, shielded windows. Fits the profile for a hardened command and control center."

I looked at her screen, then back at the timeline on mine. It fit. Close to Vance's power base, good infrastructure access, plausible commercial cover. "Okay. Assuming you're right. How do we get inside a secure Vance facility and stop trained operators from sending the kill codes?"

"Surgically," she said. "In and out. Target the primary comms antennas on the roof and the server room in the sub-basement. Cut the head off the snake before the signal fully propagates. We might not stop every field team, but we can sever the coordination, throw the entire operation into chaos. Prevent the synchronized strike."

It was desperate. Maybe suicidal. But it was the only chance we had. Staring at the cold, hard facts on our screens, the lingering mistrust between us seemed secondary to the catastrophe about to unfold. "Alright, Elena. One more time. Temporary truce. We hit this command center. Together."

"Together," she agreed, a flicker of grim determination in her eyes.

We spent the next hour planning, fueled by lukewarm coffee and adrenaline. Our resources were minimal: my pistol, hers, knives, Elena's small toolkit including breaching charges and electronic bypass tools, the element of surprise, and maybe, just maybe, a brief electronic assist from Sully if I could reach him. I sent a heavily encrypted, single-burst message via my tablet –

coordinates, target type, requested time window for a localized comms/sensor blackout. No guarantee he'd get it, or could act on it, but it was worth a try.

Getting across the city involved stealing a nondescript sedan – apologies to the owner, but needs must – and navigating the late-night traffic towards the Canal Zone. The PanIsthmus Global Logistics building was exactly as Elena described: a modern but anonymous block surrounded by high fences, cameras, and bored-looking guards.

Sully came through. Right on schedule, the external camera feeds flickered and died, and the main gate's electronic lock buzzed open for precisely thirty seconds. We drove straight through, abandoning the car near a loading dock, and used Elena's bypass tool on a service entrance.

Inside, dim emergency lights glowed. Silent corridors stretched before us. According to Elena's intel sourced from a disgruntled former employee, the comms center was on the top floor, servers in the sub-basement – connected via hardened conduits. Splitting up was risky, but faster.

"Roof access first," Elena decided. "Cut the antennas, limit their broadcast range even if we don't get the servers."

We moved upwards via the emergency stairs, encountering two guards. They went down quickly, silently, victims of Elena's thrown knife and my silenced pistol. Reaching the roof access door, Elena worked on the electronic lock while I covered the stairwell. The door clicked open.

The rooftop bristled with antennas, satellite dishes, microwave relays. Two more guards patrolled the perimeter. We took them out from the shadows, then moved to the primary broadcast arrays. Elena placed compact thermite charges – designed to melt, not explode – onto the critical junctions.

"Thirty second fuse," she whispered, activating them. "Let's go for the basement."

Back down the stairs, moving fast now. We could hear faint alarms starting somewhere in the building – maybe the guards missed a check-in. Sub-basement access was through a reinforced door marked 'Server Maintenance'. This lock was tougher, but Elena bypassed it.

The server room was frigid, filled with rows of humming racks, blinking lights. Two operators sat at consoles, headsets on, barking codes, oblivious until we burst in. One reached for a sidearm, but he was too slow. I dropped him. The other lunged for a panic button. Elena intercepted him with a brutal efficiency that spoke volumes about her training, slamming his head against the console. He slumped, unconscious or worse.

On the main screen: maps of Central America, flashing icons, streams of outgoing encrypted data. Operation Serpiente Emplumada was launching now.

"The servers! All of them!" Elena yelled, pulling out more charges.

No time for surgical strikes. We smashed coolant lines, ripped out fiber optic cables, placed explosive charges directly onto the main server racks and backup power units. As Elena set the timers – fifteen seconds – I sprayed the consoles with automatic fire from a guard's dropped weapon, shattering screens, destroying keyboards.

"Move!" We sprinted back towards the stairwell just as the first charges detonated behind us – muffled booms, the smell of burning electronics. We pounded down the stairs, heading for the ground floor service entrance where we came in.

More alarms blared now. Shouts from above. We burst out into the loading dock area just as multiple Panama National

## CHAPTER 10

Police vehicles, sirens screaming, screeched to a halt outside the main gate we'd left open. Someone inside must have hit a silent alarm linked directly to them.

"Split up!" Elena yelled, already veering left towards the perimeter fence. "Meet at the rendezvous if you make it!"

I went right, scrambling over crates, plunging back into the labyrinthine streets of Panama City's industrial zone. Behind me, I heard more sirens converging on the Vance subsidiary building, maybe some gunfire as police encountered remaining security.

Later, hiding in the shadows of a dockside warehouse, catching my breath, I risked turning on a cheap portable radio I'd boosted. News bulletins were already crackling about a major incident, explosion, possible terrorist activity at the PanIsthmus Logistics facility. Then, buried in the garbled Spanish, a mention of widespread communication failures reported by 'unspecified regional authorities', confusion, canceled alerts...

We'd done it. We'd cut the head off the snake, at least for tonight. Operation Serpiente Emplumada was crippled, the synchronized coup attempts likely aborted in chaos. It was a victory, hard-won, bloody. But Vance was still out there. Lars was still out there. And my anonymous client... their motives remained dangerously unclear. The fire was out, for now. But the embers glowed hot, and the shadows in Panama felt deeper than ever.

# Chapter 11

Finding anonymity in Panama City after blowing up a corporate communications hub wasn't easy. Sirens still echoed faintly across the humid sprawl as I ditched the hotwired car near the sprawling Mercado de Mariscos, the pungent smell of fish and diesel fumes momentarily masking the lingering scent of burnt electronics on my clothes. I needed off the street, needed a place without security cameras or desk clerks who remembered faces. I ended up in Calidonia, a chaotic district of crumbling tenements, blasting music, and watchful eyes that weren't necessarily police or syndicate, just wary locals. A grimy pension that rented rooms by the hour, no questions asked, cash upfront, seemed like the least bad option.

The room was small, stiflingly hot, furnished with a sagging cot and a single flickering fluorescent tube. Felt depressingly familiar. I wedged a chair under the flimsy doorknob, showered quickly in lukewarm water that tasted of rust, and examined the data card again on the burner tablet. Operation Serpiente Emplumada. Crippled, hopefully, but the players were still on the board. Vance. Zukhov, somewhere. Jaguar. My unknown client. And Elena.

She hadn't made the rendezvous point we'd hastily agreed on near the edge of the Canal Zone. Did she get caught? Did she simply decide splitting up was permanent? Or was she pursuing her own agenda, maybe trying to leverage the chaos we created to find definitive proof about Dr. Ramirez? Her reappearance, her skills, her certainty about the command center location... it felt too convenient now, looking back. Another layer of suspicion settled over my already weary mind.

Who could I trust? Sully, maybe, though even he operated in shades of grey. Certainly not the anonymous entity who'd sent me here with half-truths and a fat bankroll. Retrieve stolen documents? More like 'kick over the anthill and see who comes running, then grab the intel that spills out'.

A floorboard creaked in the hallway outside my door. Soft, deliberate. Not the heavy tread of police or the hurried steps of other tenants. I killed the tablet screen, palmed my pistol, moved silently away from the door into the deepest shadows of the small room. The chair wedged under the knob scraped slightly as pressure was applied from outside. Then, silence.

A thin blade slid expertly into the gap between the door and the frame, probing for the cheap lock mechanism. A metallic click, soft as a sigh, and the door swung inward slowly, pushing the chair aside.

Lars stepped into the room, moving with the same silent, fluid grace I remembered from the jungle. He held his suppressed pistol loosely at his side, his pale eyes scanning the room, finding me instantly in the shadows. He didn't seem surprised.

"Leaving without saying goodbye, Kincaid?" he asked, his voice calm, almost conversational. "Poor form."

"My social graces decline when people point guns at me," I retorted, keeping my own weapon steady. "How did you find me?"

"You are predictable," Lars said simply. "You create chaos,

then seek anonymity in the nearest available sewer. This district was logical. Finding the specific room required only a little patience... and monitoring the local lowlifes who notice strangers." He took another step inside, letting the door drift closed behind him. "Impressive work at the PanIsthmus facility. My employers were... pleased with the disruption. Operation Serpiente Emplumada is effectively neutralized for the foreseeable future."

"Glad I could help your 'dissenting shareholders' out," I said, sarcasm dripping. "So why are you here? To offer a bonus?"

"I am here for the data card," he stated flatly. "The operational details are now secondary, perhaps even compromised. But the financial data, the links to Vance, the communications between Alpha and Jaguar... that remains extremely valuable. My employers require it."

"Told you before, Lars. It stays with me."

"Circumstances have changed," he argued, his tone hardening slightly. "You are exposed. Vance knows who you are and what you've done. Jaguar's people in Costa Rica will be hunting you relentlessly. Your own client... well, let's just say relying on their benevolence might be unwise."

"What do you know about my client?" I asked sharply.

Lars allowed himself another one of his fleeting, cold smiles. "Perhaps more than you do. Think about it, Kincaid. Someone hires you, an outsider with a certain reputation, for a vague retrieval mission. They provide you with highly secure communication, substantial funds, but minimal actual intel. Your contact conveniently dies just after pointing you towards a paramilitary base disguised as a nature reserve. Inside, you don't find dusty old documents; you find detailed plans for a major regional destabilization plot, something far bigger than your stated mission."

He paused, letting the implications sink in. "Doesn't it seem... orchestrated? As if someone wanted you to find those plans? As if they knew precisely where the operation's nerve center was, knew you had the skills to potentially disrupt it, and used you as a deniable weapon against Vance and Zukhov?"

The pieces clicked, forming an ugly picture. The anonymity. The specific phone. The conveniently located data card I 'found'. The way the mission morphed from simple retrieval to stopping a multi-national coup plot. "You think my client is your employers?" I asked, the thought leaving a bitter taste. "Using me as a cutout?"

"Possible," Lars conceded. "Or perhaps another player entirely, using both you and my employers. The world is full of competing interests, Kincaid. What matters is that you were manipulated. Sent in blind, pointed like a weapon, expected perhaps to fail but cause enough disruption in the process. Your survival is likely inconvenient for them now." He took another step closer. "They used you. They won't protect you. Hand over the card. My employers can offer... protection. A way out."

Protection from his employers? The ones who likely wanted Zukhov and Vance out of the way so they could take over? It was trading one set of sharks for another. "Nice try, Lars. But I prefer to choose my own poison."

His eyes hardened. "A poor choice." He moved then, not raising his pistol, but lunging forward with surprising speed, aiming a disabling strike at my gun hand.

I sidestepped, bringing my pistol up, but he was too close, deflecting my arm, slamming his other hand into my already bruised ribs. Pain exploded behind my eyes. We crashed against the flimsy wall, grappling in the confined space. He was strong, fast, brutally efficient. Years younger than me, uninjured. I used leverage, desperation, driving my knee into his thigh, breaking his hold momentarily. I shoved him back, creating space, fired once – not to kill, but aiming for his shoulder, trying to disable him.

He twisted, the shot going wide, punching a hole in the thin wall. He came back at me, knife suddenly appearing in his hand, a thin stiletto blade glittering in the dim light. He slashed, cutting my arm – the same one injured on the yacht. I kicked out, catching his knee, sending him stumbling back against the cot.

Before he could recover, I grabbed the only weapon available – the rickety wooden chair I'd wedged against the door earlier – and brought it down hard across his shoulders. Wood splintered, the chair disintegrated, but the impact knocked him off balance.

He snarled, lunging again, knife flashing. I ducked under the wild slash, pivoted, and slammed the door open, stumbling out into the dingy hallway. No time to finish the fight; getting out was the priority.

Lars recovered quickly, appearing in the doorway, pistol raised. I didn't hesitate, firing two shots back down the hallway – not aiming at him, but at the bare bulb overhead and the grimy window at the far end, plunging the corridor into near total darkness, showering the floor with glass.

I scrambled down the narrow, rickety stairs, hearing Lars curse behind me but not immediately following – likely assessing the situation, unwilling to charge blindly into the dark. I hit the street, melting into the late-night foot traffic of El Chorrillo, heart pounding, arm bleeding again, ribs screaming.

Lars was right about one thing. I had been manipulated. The job, the client, maybe even Elena's convenient appearance…

layers upon layers of deception. Retrieve documents? No. My real mission, assigned unknowingly, had been to blow Serpiente Emplumada wide open, exposing Vance, hurting Zukhov, serving the agenda of some unseen player who now probably considered me a loose end.

I still had the data card. But the knowledge it contained felt toxic now, tainted by the realization that I was just a pawn in someone else's lethal game. Who was the client? What was their real endgame? And how many more layers of this conspiracy were still hidden in the shadows? The questions swirled in my head as I disappeared into the Panama City night, more hunted, and more uncertain, than ever before.

## Chapter 12

Panama faded behind me not with a clean break, but like a persistent fever finally receding, leaving behind aches, chills, and a lingering sense of disorientation. Getting out involved none of the relative ease of arrival. Vance's security apparatus, now fully alerted, had eyes everywhere. Lars's warning echoed in my head – my survival was likely inconvenient for whoever pulled the strings. Airports were suicide, official border crossings equally risky under any alias I currently possessed. It took five miserable days, working my way north through the Darien Gap fringes with guides whose silence I bought with the last remnants of the client's blood money, then hopping local buses, coastal freighters, and eventually talking my way onto a leaky fishing trawler running snapper up the coast towards Mobile. The journey was a blur of stifling bus cabins, pitching decks that smelled of fish guts and diesel, shared rice and beans, and constant, gnawing paranoia. Every stranger's glance felt like surveillance, every police siren like the closing of a net.

Stepping back onto Florida soil felt less like a homecoming and more like returning to the scene of a previous crime. The air was familiar, the specific weight of the humidity, the scent of salt and mangroves carried on the breeze. But I felt changed, disconnected. I made my way south cautiously, avoiding high-

## CHAPTER 12

ways, sticking to back roads, finally reaching the marina under the cover of darkness, slipping aboard the Sea Witch like a ghost reclaiming its haunt.

The old boat welcomed me with familiar creaks and smells. Settling into the cramped cabin felt like pulling on a worn, comfortable glove, but the comfort was illusory. The world outside had intruded, violated the sanctuary I'd tried to build here. The warrants were still active. Zukhov was still out there. Croft still played philanthropist nearby. Vance pulled strings from Panama. Lars, or his employers, were hunting the data card I still carried. And Elena... where did she fit? Ally? Rival? Pawn? Just another casualty? Her face, furious and disillusioned in the jungle gloom, lingered in my memory.

Weeks passed. I let the Florida sun try to bake the chill out of my bones, let the rhythm of the tides soothe the jagged edges of my nerves. I worked on the boat, sanding, varnishing, tinkering, needing the mindless physical labor. But the peace wouldn't settle. Lars's words echoed: Manipulated. Pointed like a weapon. Who was the client? Why hire me for a document retrieval that turned into stopping a multi-national coup attempt? What was their real endgame?

I spent hours below deck with the burner tablet Sully had insisted I take from his safehouse and the data card, shielding the glow from the portholes. I contacted Sully via our most secure, slowest channel – encrypted bursts bounced off multiple satellites.

"You look like hell warmed over, Jack," his voice crackled eventually through the tiny receiver, accompanied by grainy video. "Heard things got noisy down south."

"You could say that," I replied drily. "Operation Serpiente Emplumada is offline. For now." I filled him in on the command center strike, the escape, the confrontation with Lars, the rival operative's claims about my client.

Sully listened, his expression grim. "Lars... sounds like one of 'The Competition'. Ex-Stasi, Scandinavian mercs, corporate espionage types mostly. Ruthless. If they say they want the data, they won't stop." He paused. "And he thinks your client set you up?"

"Painted a convincing picture," I admitted. "Said they knew I'd find the Serpiente plans, used me to disrupt Vance and Zukhov."

"Possible," Sully mused. "Extremely risky, letting intel like that potentially fall into your hands, but possible. If they wanted plausible deniability and maximum disruption..." He sighed. "The problem is, we still don't know who 'they' are. Your client covered their tracks impeccably. The initial payment originated from a ghost account in Luxembourg, vanished immediately after transfer."

"Can you dig deeper into this Vance character? Or the Panama operation?" I asked. "Maybe find a link back?"

"Already been trying," Sully said. "Scrubbing the data card again, looking for communication fragments, metadata Varga might have missed, anything linking Vance outwards."

We worked remotely for days, Sully applying his formidable skills to the layers of data on the card, me running cross-references, searching for patterns. Mostly dead ends. Vance, Zukhov, Jaguar – their operational security was top-tier. But then Sully found something odd, buried in the encrypted financial authorizations from Vance to Jaguar.

"Recognize this routing code, Jack?" Sully asked, transmitting a short alphanumeric sequence.

It looked vaguely familiar. I dug through my own sparse notes from Book 1, the sanitized background Pym had provided on Silas Thorne's holdings, the connections I'd tentatively made to Harrison Croft. "Wait a second... that's similar to a secondary holding company Croft used. One tied to his more... speculative international investments."

"Exactly," Sully confirmed. "Not identical, but uses the same non-standard encrypted protocol, originates from the same private banking network in Zurich favored by both Croft and Vance Global Holdings. It's not conclusive proof, Jack, not even close. But it's a thread."

A thread connecting Croft in Florida directly to Vance in Panama? So they weren't just parallel syndicate financiers; they were potentially collaborators, maybe even partners in the same overarching structure. Zukhov's Florida operation and Jaguar's Central American training camp weren't separate ventures; they were branches of the same tree. A tree with very deep, very rotten roots.

"And there's more," Sully added, his voice grim. "Buried in some technical specs attached to requisitions for the Costa Rica camp – things that didn't make sense, labeled 'special projects equipment'. Cross-referenced the component numbers... it's not standard paramilitary gear, Jack. Looks more like... advanced genetic sequencing hardware. And secure bio-containment units."

Bio-tech? Genetic sequencing? What the hell was a syndicate training camp doing with that kind of equipment? It didn't fit the destabilization plot. It hinted at something else entirely, something colder, more sophisticated.

"One last thing," Sully said. "Found this symbol embedded as a watermark in some of the highest-level encrypted files from Vance – the ones authorizing the 'special projects' funding.

Doesn't match any known syndicate markings or corporate logos I have on file." He transmitted an image: a stylized serpent, coiled into an infinity loop, consuming its own tail, but with a single, stylized electronic 'node' depicted at the center of the loop.

An Ouroboros with a microchip heart. It meant nothing to me, but it felt significant, chillingly deliberate. A symbol for the real players behind Vance, behind Croft, maybe even behind Zukhov?

I leaned back in the cramped cabin, the familiar rocking of the Sea Witch doing little to soothe the fresh wave of unease. Florida felt different now. Not a refuge, just another node in a network that seemed to span continents, dealing not just in guns and coups, but maybe something far more insidious. Croft, Vance, the bio-tech, the strange symbol... the shadows were wider, deeper than I ever imagined.

Lars was still out there. Zukhov was rebuilding. Vance was plotting. Elena was a wildcard. My client remained a ghost, pulling strings for unknown reasons. And I was sitting on a boat in Florida, technically a fugitive, holding a data card full of secrets and a handful of disturbing new clues pointing towards a conspiracy that made everything before look like petty squabbles.

I looked out the porthole at the afternoon sun glinting on the water, the carefree shouts of tourists heading out on charter boats. Part of me, the smart part, screamed to provision the Sea Witch, point her bow south, and disappear into the myriad islands of the Caribbean, leave the whole damn mess behind.

But the other part, the stubborn, weary, maybe foolish part, felt the familiar pull. The unanswered questions. The faces of the dead. The chilling implication of that Ouroboros symbol.

## CHAPTER 12

The wider shadows were gathering. And like it or not, I had a feeling I was about to sail right into them. The next mission hadn't been assigned, but the coordinates were already starting to form on the map.

Can I ***send you CONSCRIPTED FOR FREE?***

Don't miss the rest of the DECLASSIFIED FILES on Amazon Now!

www.ingramcontent.com/pod-product-compliance
Lightning Source LLC
LaVergne TN
LVHW041713060526
838201LV00043B/710